"For breakfast," said Mrs Troutbeck, "we have scrambled eggs with mushrooms, cornflakes and some orange juice, which I have unfrozen.

Where's Julius?"

Mr Troutbeck called their son Julius and they all sat down to breakfast.

"For lunch today we are having sardines on toast, a roll and butter, tomatoes, and nothing for pudding.

Where's Julius?"

"Julius says he cannot have lunch with us today because he has made a little home in the other room with three chairs, the old curtains and the broom."

So Mr Troutbeck took the tray with the sardines on toast, a roll and butter, tomatoes and no pudding to the other room where Julius had made his little home out of three chairs, the old curtains and the broom.

Where's Julius?

John Burningham

RED FOX

Other books by John Burningham

ABC
Aldo
Avocado Baby
Borka
Cloudland
Come Away from the Water, Shirley
Courtney
Granpa
Harquin
Humbert
John Patrick Norman McHennessy

Mr Gumpy's Motor Car
Mr Gumpy's Outing
Oi! Get off our Train
Seasons
Simp
The Shopping Basket
Time to get out of the Bath, Shirley
Trubloff
Whadayamean
Would You Rather?

Little Books
The Baby
The Blanket
The Cupboard
The Dog
The Friend
The Rabbit
The School
The Snow

A Red Fox Book

Published by Random House Children's Books
20 Vauxhall Bridge Road, London SW1V 2SA

A division of The Random House Group Ltd
London Melbourne Sydney Auckland
Johannesburg and agencies throughout the world

Copyright © John Burningham 1986

1 3 5 7 9 10 8 6 4 2

First published in Great Britain by Jonathan Cape Ltd, 1986
This Red Fox edition 2001

Printed in Singapore by Tien Wah Press (PTE) Ltd

THE RANDOM HOUSE GROUP Limited Reg. No. 954009
www.randomhouse.co.uk

ISBN 0 09 941429 5

"I've got the lamb casserole for supper out of the oven and the potatoes in their jackets and broccoli with butter on top and for afterwards there is roly-poly pudding.

Where's Julius?"

"Julius says he cannot have supper with us just at the moment because he is digging a hole in order to get to the other side of the world."

So Mrs Troutbeck took the lamb casserole, the potatoes in their jackets and broccoli with butter on top and the roly-poly pudding for afterwards to where Julius was digging his hole.

"For breakfast there is sausage, bacon and egg, toast and marmalade and also a glass of Three-Flavour Fruit Juice.

Where's Julius?"

"Julius says he cannot have breakfast with us today because he is riding a camel to the top of the tomb of Neffatuteum which is a pyramid near the Nile in Egypt."

So Mr Troutbeck took the tray with the sausage, bacon and egg, toast and marmalade and the glass of Three-Flavour Fruit Juice – and another for the camel – to Egypt where Julius was riding to the top of the pyramid.

"For lunch there is cheese salad with celery and tomato and an orange for pudding if you want it.

Where's Julius?"

"Julius says he cannot have lunch with us just at the moment because he is cooling the hippopotamuses in the Lombo Bombo River in Central Africa, with buckets of muddy water."

So Mr Troutbeck took the tray with the cheese salad with celery and tomato and the orange for pudding to Africa where Julius was pouring buckets of muddy water on the hippopotamuses, to keep them cool.

"Here are the grilled chops for supper. There are baby carrots, garden peas and mashed potato to go with them, and an apple crumble for pudding.

Where's Julius?"

"Julius says he can't have supper with us just at the moment because he is throwing snowballs at the wolves from a sledge in which he is crossing the frozen wastes of Novosti Krosky which lies somewhere in Russia where the winters are long."

So Mrs Troutbeck took the tray with the chop, the baby carrots, garden peas and mashed potato to go with them, and an apple crumble for pudding to Novosti Krosky which lies somewhere in Russia where Julius was throwing snowballs at the wolves.

"For breakfast we are having boiled eggs, toast and marmalade and the Tropical Fruit Juice that you wanted.

Where's Julius?"

"Julius says he cannot have breakfast with us just at the moment because he is watching the sunrise from the top of the Changa Benang mountains somewhere near Tibet."

So Mr Troutbeck
took the tray with
the boiled egg,
toast and marmalade
and the Tropical
Fruit Juice
to the top of the
Changa Benang
mountains
somewhere near Tibet,
where Julius was
watching the sunrise.

"For lunch we are having spaghetti bolognese with lettuce and cucumber. For pudding there is plum duff.

Where's Julius?"

"Julius says he can't have lunch with us at the moment because he is on a raft which he has made from pieces of wood and old oil drums and he is about to shoot the rapids on the Chico Neeko River somewhere in Peru in South America."

So Mrs Troutbeck took the tray with the spaghetti bolognese, the lettuce and cucumber and the plum duff to the Chico Neeko River in South America where Julius was about to shoot the rapids on his raft.

"For supper today there is Lancashire hot-pot,
and steamed pudding for afterwards.

Is Julius building a home out of old curtains,
chairs and the broom?

Digging a hole to get to the other side of the world?

Riding a camel up a pyramid?

Cooling the hippos that stand in the
Lombo Bombo River?

Throwing snowballs at wolves in Novosti Krosky
where the winters are long?

Is he climbing the Changa Benang mountains,
or shooting the rapids on the Chico Neeko River
in South America?

Perhaps he is helping the young owls to learn
to fly in the trees at the end of the road
or tucking the polar bears in their beds
somewhere in Antarctica?"

"Betty," said Mr Troutbeck, "tonight Julius
is having supper at home."